MY BROTHER

Sandals
are
cool!

SUPER
BROTHER!

He's a
STAR!

F.A.B.

My
Mate

He's
GREAT!

I could
have done
better with
my sandals
on!

MY BROTHER
A PICTURE CORGI BOOK 978 0 552 55551 7

First published in Great Britain by Doubleday,
an imprint of Random House Children's Books
A Random House Group Company

Doubleday edition published 2007
Picture Corgi edition published 2008

1 3 5 7 9 10 8 6 4 2

Copyright © AET Browne, 2007

The right of Anthony Browne to be identified as the author
and illustrator of this work has been asserted in accordance
with the Copyright, Designs and Patents Act 1988.

Picture Corgi Books are published by
Random House Children's Books,
61–63 Uxbridge Road, London W5 5SA
A division of The Random House Group Ltd

www.kidsatrandomhouse.co.uk   www.rbooks.co.uk

Addresses for companies within The Random House Group Limited
can be found at: www.randomhouse.co.uk/offices.htm

THE RANDOM HOUSE GROUP Limited Reg. No. 954009

A CIP catalogue record for this book is available
from the British Library.

Printed and bound in Singapore

With thanks to
Iona Scott's class
at the British School
in the Netherlands
for inspiring this book

To my
brother
Michael
who isn't cool!
(he's warm!)

Anthony Browne
MY BROTHER

Picture Corgi

My brother
is really COOL.

cool jump

He's a GREAT jumper,

cool climbing

cool Kong

a
TERRIFIC
climber,

cool goal →

and he scores FANTASTIC goals!

He's REALLY cool, my brother.

cool pants

and he's got
MASSIVE
muscles.

He can run so FAST that . . .

...he can FLY!

Yes, my brother
is really COOL.

cool
chair →

My brother's read
HUNDREDS of books,

cool knight

cool giant

cool soldier

and he writes
BRILLIANT stories.

cool wolf

He can draw
ANYTHING,

and he can blow AMAZING bubbles.
He's REALLY COOL, my brother.

My brother is a WILD rock singer,

cool shirt

cool suit

cool
medallion

COOL

and a DAZZLING disco dancer.

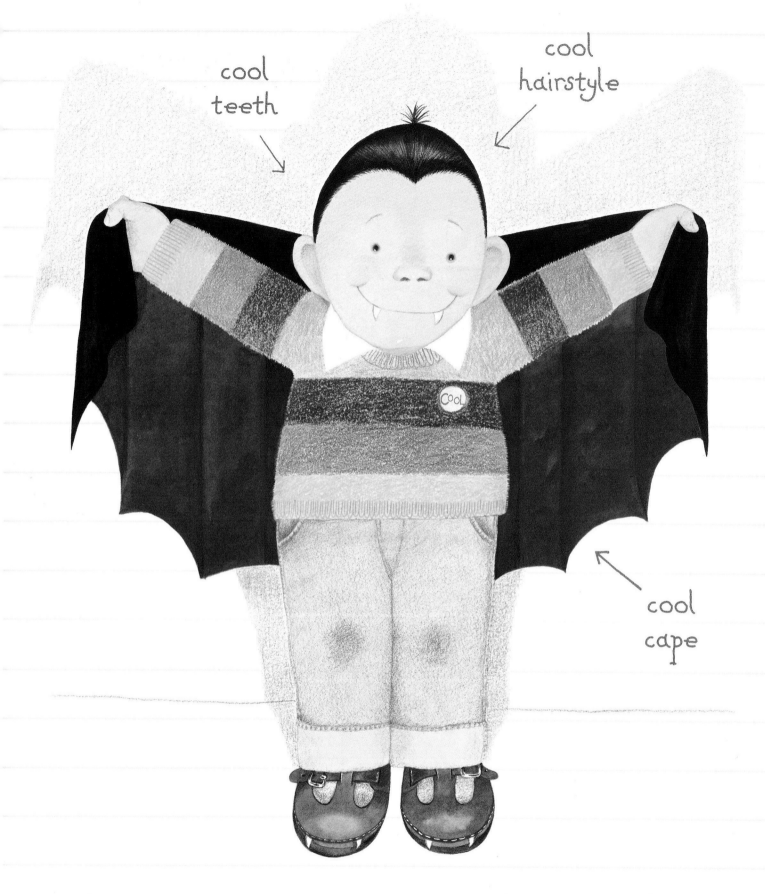

Sometimes he can be VERY SCARY,

and he can even WHISTLE!
My brother is SO cool.

My brother STANDS UP to bullies,

and SITS DOWN
on monsters.

cool ears →

cool shades ←

cool whiskers →

COOL

cool tail ↓

REALLY cool sandals ↓

As a matter of fact, my brother is a REAL COOL CAT.

And guess what . . .

I'M COOL TOO!

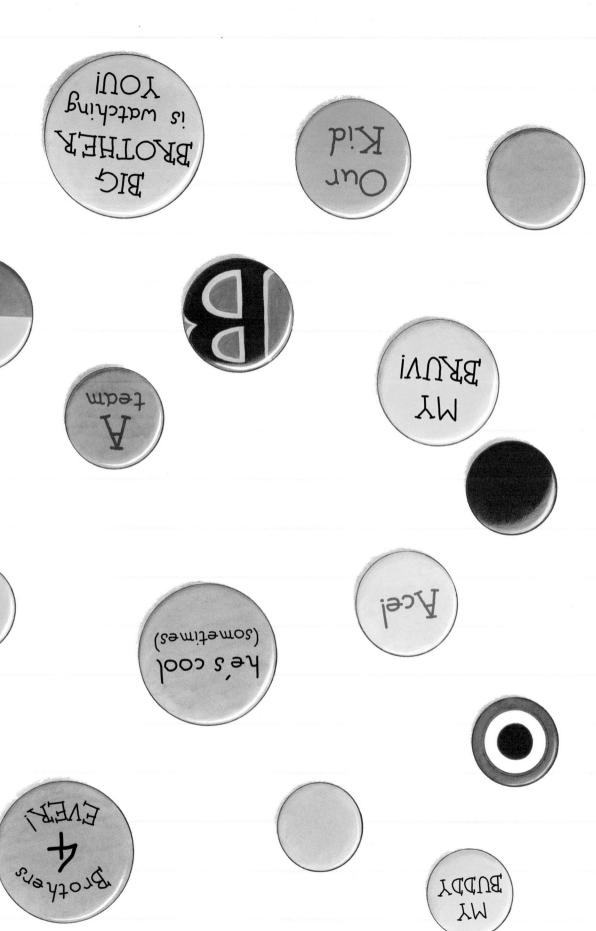

Sandals
are
cool!

SUPER
BROTHER!

He's a
STAR!

F.A.B.

He's
GREAT!

My
Mate

I could
have done
better with
my sandals
on!

Other books by Anthony Browne

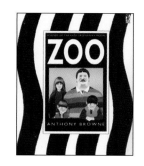

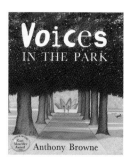

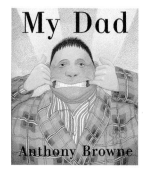

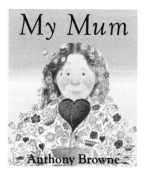

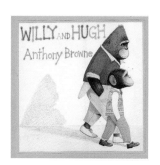